Edward Templeman

Poems: Narrative and Descriptive

Written in England and India

Edward Templeman

Poems: Narrative and Descriptive
Written in England and India

ISBN/EAN: 9783337158132

Printed in Europe, USA, Canada, Australia, Japan

Cover: Foto ©Andreas Hilbeck / pixelio.de

More available books at **www.hansebooks.com**

POEMS:

NARRATIVE AND DESCRIPTIVE.

𝔚ritten in 𝔈ngland and 𝔈ndia.

BY THE

REV. EDWARD TEMPLEMAN,

RECTOR OF PITCHCOTT, AYLESBURY, AND CHAPLAIN OF SCHORNE COLLEGE
LATE VICAR OF HIGHAM FERRERS AND CHELVESTON
WITH CALDECOTE ANNEXED ;
AND CHAPLAIN RETIRED LIST H.M.I.S.

LONDON :
ELLIOT STOCK, 62, PATERNOSTER ROW, E.C
1891.

PREFACE.

In publishing this little work, I am very conscious that its contents will not endure the test of severe criticism ; still, I venture to hope it will be read with kindly interest by many friends who have expressed themselves favourably of some of the poems in the volume which they have read. Some were published in India, whilst others have never before been printed. It was my happy lot to be educated at a school where the Bible and the Prayer-book were carefully and devoutly taught, most especially by a young and earnest master and clergyman, who died at a very early age, and whose death at such a time made a deep and lasting impression on a schoolboy's mind. To the example and teaching of this good young master, I am indebted, I believe, for early religious impressions. During the last few years of my life I have been engaged in similar work to his, and, under the guidance of one who knows well the value of God's Word for young and old alike, and to whom, with much esteem, I have ventured to dedicate this volume. I have been endeavouring to interest schoolboys in the best of all books, and the one which can alone be called holy, and which, when its beautiful lessons are brought home to our hearts by the Spirit of God, can make us wise unto salvation through faith which is in Christ Jesus our Lord.

CONTENTS.

———•◦•———

SCHORNE COLLEGE.*

NEAR a small village in our happy land,
  Nestled beneath an emerald grassy hill,
Uprose, as touched by wise magician's hand,
  A college founded by the Warden's skill—

The school and *home* of many a gallant boy,
  Moulded and trained by vigorous master's
      mind
To love the pure, abhor the base alloy,
  Reject the evil, choose the truth refined,

Pure as the water from Schorne's well-known well,†
  The truth as found in Holy Writ is taught ;
And day by day at sound of chiming bell
  The Saviour's praise is sung, His mercy sought.

---

* Schorne College is situated in the village of North
Marston, Bucks, a village (including the college, which has
greatly increased the population) of about 800 people, with
a beautiful church, in which her Majesty the Queen has
placed a stained glass east window.

† There is a well in the village celebrated for its tonic
chalybeate water, and called Sir John Schorne's well.

I

He who in wisdom first devised the plan,
   And to completion brought his cherished work,
Has by *his life* taught boys to play the man,
   And ne'er in honest toil or *play* to shirk.

Well disciplined in school, in pastimes trained
   Hardness to suffer, temper to control,
In the world's fight Schorne boys have honour
     gained,
   In its keen race unfaltering reached the goal.

From many a land, across the pathless sea,
   From office desks, from ship and regiment,
Old Schornians' thoughts flow back unceasingly
   To the loved school where their best days were
     spent.

Parents and boys to God will offer prayer
   For him whose generous heart and purpose
     true
By earnest thought and unremitting care
   Oped learning's fields to them, and ' pastures
     new.'

Long may Schorne flourish, and the master mind
   Its vigour long retain to rule and guide !
And long may scholars 'neath its rooftree find
   Man's teaching, by God's Spirit sanctified !

REMINISCENCE OF CLAYDON RECTORY.

JUNE 1, 1891.

THE first of summer days, a season meet
For opening flowers, and the voices sweet
Of woodland nightingale and cooing dove,
Their songs upraising, and blue sky above.
Soothed and refreshed our souls, as once again,
Some by grassy lanes, others by train,
From Oxford's crowded streets their footsteps
      bent
To this loved spot, where students oft have spent,
From studies freed, a peaceful afternoon
Beneath the beech-trees' shade in leafy June ;*
Spent hours of sweet communion, fervent prayer
To Him whose Spirit surely led them there :
Who guides the thoughts and moves the lips of
      those
From whom pure thoughts and ripened wisdom
      flows.
There first to welcome us, with others, came
The best-beloved, Sir Harry, still the same

---

* The Oxford Union for Private Prayer meets once a
year, generally on Trinity Tuesday, at Claydon Rectory,
close to the well-known seat—Claydon House—of the Right
Hon. Sir Harry Verney, Bart.

In heart and purpose, God all-trusting, true—
The same brave soul as in past days we knew,
When well-nigh forty years ago we knelt
Near this same spot, and Christ's sweet presence
    felt ;
Never more loved, never more honoured,
Than now, when *ninety snows* are on his head !
Our host, the Rector, 'neath the trees of yew,
Spoke words of counsel wise and wisdom true,
And from God's Book good lessons for us
    drew.
Then one of India his experience told—
When lonely, in that far-off land of old,
The thought that prayer was offered by a band,
A brotherhood, in the dear Fatherland,
Would soothe his heart and nerve him for the
    fight,
And cheer his spirit through the darkest night.
Another Senior of his brother tells
Who the same comfort felt in the Seychelles.
From bright Australia and New Zealand, friends
Unknown before, from the world's distant ends,
Had come to spend with us this happy day,
And earnestly entreated all to pray
For the lone wanderers in bush or track,
Lest they should faith and godly fervour lack.
Then last and late, but only not *too* late,
Came one his thrilling story to relate !

The life of him by whose wise thought and care
Our gathering for mutual help and prayer
Was founded ; who with brothers sought
Mutual aid, and to completion brought
This work which lasts, and with God's blessing
      thrives,
Sustaining hope and strengthening anxious lives,
As was our Founder's, faithful to the end,
Striving with Mussulman and rallying friend !*
With deepest interest we heard how Trench had
      toiled
For Jesus, and how Satan's power had foiled
In England and in India ; and how died
His only hope his Saviour crucified.

    *   *   *   *   *

Then as the summer sun sank in the west,
And Nature lulled herself to peaceful rest,
We homeward bent our way, praying that we
The lessons taught to-day so earnestly
Might by God's Spirit give us grace to try
Like saints departed live, and in Christ die !

* Bishop Trench, late Bishop of Lahore, died of sunstroke at Muscat, where he had gone to preach to the
Mussulmans alone, after noble service again and again
renewed in India, the North-West, and Punjaub and Afghan
frontier.

OUR LILIAN, THE SOLDIER'S CHILD.

It frequently happened during the great Indian Mutiny, in 1857-58, that the Sepoys broke into the English burial-grounds and cemeteries and destroyed the gravestones of those who had been buried there. This cruel act had been committed in the cemetery of a station in which I was chaplain towards the end of the rebellion. A lady, the wife of a Major—whose little daughter had been buried in my churchyard—was anxious to know if her child's grave had been mutilated, whereupon I searched for it and found it, the grave itself only slightly trampled on, which was not always the case, but the little cross over the grave broken as described in the following poem, which was founded on this circumstance and published in the *Anglo-Indian Magazine*, from which I now transcribe it. I am indebted to the good Dr. Kaye, the late Principal of Bishop's College, Calcutta, who was then acting editor of the magazine, which was principally for soldiers, for one or two emendations he kindly made for me.

PART I.

Our Lilian was our only child,
  The nursling of a day;
Upon our life she sweetly smiled,
  Then gently passed away.
She was not *given* to cheer our life,
  God took her back again
Ere sin or this world's cruel strife
  Had ever caused her pain.

Oh, bitter trial with her to part,
  The *one* child of our love!
But the richest treasure of our heart
  We know is *safe* above.
A soldier's child was Lilian;
  And, in our gallant band,
Full many a rough but honest man
  Would lead her by his hand.
The favourite of our camp was she ;
  With childhood's prattle gay,
Her cheery laughter merrily
  Rang out the livelong day.
And I had brought her very far
  Across the pathless deep ;
And I little thought the child of war
  So soon would fall asleep.
We landed upon India's shore,
  And thanked our Father God
That, our long voyage safely o'er,
  Once more on land we trod.
And up we travelled many a mile
  O'er bright and burning sand,
And Lilian would often smile
  At the sights of this strange land !
We journeyed on our slow long way
  Until we reached the spot
Where, camping, Lilian's father lay—
  The partner of my lot.

He clasped *me* closely to his breast,
    Then fondled in his arms
His child ; she was the loveliest,'
    The dearest of his charms.
Ah ! little did he know the fate
    Impending o'er her head,
Nor could he see death's angel wait
    Close by to strike her dead.
She was a babe in arms when he
    Kissed her and said good-bye,
But now she reached up to his knee—
    Had grown, he said, *so high !*
None but a father's tongue could tell
    His joy, as he smoothed her hair,
And none knew how his heart with love did swell
    But those who have *felt* it *there.*
Soon came the heavy Indian scourge,
    And full many swept away,
And for young and old a funeral dirge
    Was wailed forth every day !
Our Lilian with others fell
    Beneath death's withering hand ;
But she is now we know full well
    In a better, happier land.
When I think how sweetly in death she smiled
    With tears my eyes are dim ;
But 'twas Jesus called our little child,
    And we leave her now with Him.

PART II.—LILIAN'S GRAVE.

The red sun sank down in the west,
  The heavy day was passed,
And I, most bitterly oppressed,
  Half wished it were my last.
The day was gone, but with its close
  My anguish did not cease,
Nor could kind words or the acts of those
  I loved most give me peace.
They helped me well in my sad trial,
  And led me to the spot
Where from their labours rest awhile
  The dead and the forgot.
Upon his strong, stout arm I leant,
  The bravest of the brave,
But the *strong* man's strength was almost spent
  Beside his loved child's grave.
I felt him quiver in each limb
  Like a frail aspen tree,
For sorrow's cup, filled to the brim,
  Made the man *womanly*.
It was natural he should be *my stay*,
  As he had been all along,
Through many a rough and stormy day,
  When weak I knew *him* strong.
But when we stood in twilight gloom,
  With hearts o'er-full to speak,

Beside our darling's new-made tomb,
  Both weak and strong were weak,
And when they lowered the cruel ropes
  And the little coffin shell,
It seemed to us that all our hopes
  Were buried there as well.
" Ashes to ashes, dust to dust"—
  And must we leave thee there ?
God be our confidence and trust,
  And let us not despair !
Oh ! trial of trials, in a foreign land
  To lose our brightest gem ;
Oh ! hope of hopes, that at God's right hand
  She decks His diadem.
In a strange but hallowed spot she'll sleep
  Beneath the mango's shade,
And watchful angels *guard* will keep
  Where the *soldier's child* is laid.
And there are other graves beside
  In that still sleeping place,
Of those who've died in manhood's pride
  Or run a longer race,
So when she rises at the last
  She'll not be all alone
To hear the archangel's trumpet's blast,
  And stand before the throne !
With thoughts as these we left her there,
  To sleep in peaceful rest,

Returning to a world of care
  Resigned to God's behest.
Then o'er her grave a stone we placed,
  And o'er the stone a cross,
On which a few fond words we traced,
  Which spoke our hope and loss.
We wrote her age, her day of birth,
  Her own beloved name ;
How soon her spirit left this earth,
  Returning *whence* it came.
In holy words of Him we told
  Who gathers in His arms
The lambs, and in His breast will fold
  The little ones from harm.

   *   *   *   *   *

Years rolled away.   I came again
  To the well-remembered spot ;
But who can tell the grief and pain
  Which then fell to my lot ?
Both were destroyed, both cross and stone,
  The sacred grave defiled
By those who ne'er had pity shown
  To woman, babe, or child.
It matters not ; my memory
  Retains that lovely face,
And no rude hand of enemy
  Can tear it from *that* place.

FRAGMENTS.

The following lines were published in the same magazine. They will, I hope, be read with indulgence, as they were written when the author had not yet reached his twentieth year, and are selected from a poem of upwards of five hundred lines.

I.

Who has not learnt that hoarded wealth
    And all the treasures of this earth
    Are in themselves but little worth?
To keep the soul in perfect health
    Should be our care; to elevate
Our thoughts to joys above the earth,
    And train them for a holier state;
To seek bright jewels in the mine
    Of virtue, love, and righteousness,
Treasures which will the clearer shine
    When all else fades to nothingness.

II.

Be this ambition's noblest aim,
    Raise up thy soul nor linger here,
    For tho' thou art a sojourner
Upon this earth, tho' from it came
    Thy body, yet thyself, thy soul,
Is of a nature loftier.
    Nor should this world its thoughts control,

Since it to realms above may soar,
　And to its home in thought can flee,
Speeding thitherward before
　It leaves this world of mystery.

III.

'Twill burst its prison bars at times,
　Each thought of earth will cast aside,
　And, upward soaring, swiftly glide
Far hence away to happier climes.
　And holy thoughts wing it along
O'er distant lands and oceans wide
　To that blest spot where sin or wrong
Have never left their withering trace.
　Ah! who has not imagined this?
Who has not pictured such a place,
　Where all is love and perfect bliss?

IV.

He is a heartless, soulless man
　Who does not often spend his time
　In thinking of that happy clime
Where joy first was, and love began;
　For there our souls *must* seek their peace,
In homes above, in realms sublime.
　Why dread we aught which can release
Our spirits from their home of clay?
　We should not dread Death's hand; 'twill ope
Heaven's pearly gates—perhaps to-day—
　And more than realize our hope.

V.

How transient are the joys of earth !
    How soon its pleasures fade away !
    Our life is like an April day,
With hours of mingled pain and mirth ;
    A brief while we may happy be ,
And feel in spirit light and gay,
    The next borne down with misery.
Fast fleeting is our life below,
    Where light is ever tinged with shade,
Each rarest joy is mixed with woe,
    Where a daily debt to sin is paid.

VI.

Not so with things in heaven above—
    They never change, nor die, nor fade ;
    There all is life, and all is made
To shine and bloom perpetually.
    Oh ! lift your thoughts to heaven, and know
That all things there are perfect made
    As all was once on earth below
Till man fell from perfection, and
    This world lost of its brightness then,
And sin's fell curse spread o'er the land
    And brought disease and woe to men.

VII.

Is there the man who does not hope
    In mansions of the skies to live ?

Breathes there a soul who does not give
His fond imagination scope
   To think on spiritual life above
Where we in perfect joy may live ?
   Will not your fancy sometimes rove
And picture scenes of endless bliss,
   Of joy unmixed with grief or pain ?
Ah ! yes, we sometimes think of this,
   But too soon turn to earth again.

VIII.

Why are our thoughts so much on earth ?
   Ah ! why not oftener fixed on heaven?
   Because our thoughts are too much given
To cling to aught of earthly birth,
   Tho' it be stained with fault and sin.
Yet are there those who well have striven
   Nature to conquer, who begin
' To be not of the world '; and they
   Find true joys here, since they alone
Look on this life as 'twere the way
   To bring us to a better one.

IX.—SOLITUDE.

It may be strange, but I have found,
   When wandering on some lonely hill
   Or listening to the brawling rill,
My thoughts made peaceful by its sound,

The purest pleasures earth can give,
   And seem in happiness to live;
As one who dwells in spirit-land,
   And the feathered choir which round me˙sing
Seem flitting like a fairy band
   To waft off sadness on their wings.

X.

And it is not always *solitude*
   Brings melancholy to our hearts;
   For sometimes lessons it imparts
Productive of the highest good.
   'Tis then the mind, tho' hard as steel,
With gentlest, kindliest feelings starts,
   And worldliest souls most deeply feel
The love they owe to Him who spread
   The myriad beauties which they see
Around their path, who lifts the head
   Of those sunk in despondency.

XI.

Oh! how I love that peaceful hour
   When twilight steals upon the earth,
   And stars shine forth of heavenly birth!
How sweetly sleeps each drooping flower,
   Its leaves refreshed with evening dew!
And every plant upon the earth
   Is decked out in its gayest hue.

The sweetest of all times to muse,
　When thoughts will stray to noblest themes,
And fancy, uncontrolled, will choose
　To lull our minds with pleasant dreams.

XII.

These are the hours when we have felt
　The change from bitterness to peace,
　And from oppression find release;
Then we with thoughts devout have knelt
　Before our Father, and outpoured
Our hearts to Him who gives us ease;
　These are the hours when we have soared
In meditation up from earth
　To glorious mansions far above,
And then first known of that new birth,
　A love for heaven, and heavenly love.

XIII.

As is it not when we have been
　Passing our time in solitude,
　Then most in meditative mood
Looking on Nature's loveliest scene
　By mountain, rill, or rugged coast,
We've known that this world's vaunted good
　Is worthless, if our souls be lost.
Is it not true that we have loved
　To think of heaven as happiness?
If by such thoughts we have been moved,
　Let us thank God for loneliness.

THE RUINS OF EGYPTIAN THEBES.

In the Christmas vacation of my first year at Oxford, when not yet twenty years old, I wrote a poem for the Newdigate, and although a better man gained the prize, the information I acquired, in reading and research, was of much advantage to me, and enabled me to take an enhanced interest in Egypt, when in the providence of God I passed through that country on my way to India.

As time flows on with restless stream each day,
He hurries fast our fleeting years away,
And sweeps us on to the unbounded sea
Till all is lost in vast eternity.
There has he borne past ages, thither rolled
Those who by might the ancient world controlled;
There swept those heroes in whose breasts beat
    high
The love of war and high-souled chivalry!
Where are those potentates whose voice alone
Could marshal armies to defend their throne—
Whose countless warriors waited their command
To march and sweep the foeman from their land?
Where are they now? Passed to that silent shore
Where time had borne their noble sires before.
Bold though they were, and powerful to withstand
The foe in battle met, still by Time's hand,
Conquered, they fell; like as the earliest flowers,
Ere they have oped their buds a few brief hours,

By some rough blast are swiftly swept aside,
So fell these men, and vanished all their pride :
Their noblest works have shared the destined lot
All mortal things must have, each beauteous spot,
Though decked in splendour *now*, the power hath
    not
To elevate the mind or charm the eye
It once possessed in ages long passed by.
Those cities once the glory of the earth,
Where heroes dwelt, who from their very birth
Had been imbued with courage to defend,
In danger's hour, their country or their friend,
Have fallen beneath Time's ruthless hand. Decay,
And of their splendour lingers but a ray,
Yet still remain their ruins to declare
What beauty and magnificence were there !
O mighty Thebes ! when Homer sang of thee,
He then thy power extolled, and majesty.*
Of jewels laid up in palaces he told,
Of gifts of silver, ornaments of gold,
In rich profusion ; sang of warriors bold
Who through thy hundred gates, when war arose,
Drove out their thousand chariots to oppose
Those who had dared to lift a hostile hand
Against a Theban and the Theban's land.
And naught save Homer's muse, with tone sublime,
Can rightly hymn thy praise, whom envious Time

* *Vide* Homer, ' Odyssey,' Book iv. 125 : ' Iliad,' ix. 381.

Hath not *all* conquered yet; still through the plain
On every side thy monuments remain,
To point to us how Egypt's bravery stood
Mistress of all beneath her power subdued.
Imagination tries, and tries in vain,
To justly sing the splendours of the plain—
To paint this 'wildering scene the loftiest mind
May contemplate each hallowed spot, and find
Its thoughts in wonder lost and solemn awe,
Until it deems the universal law
Of Nature rules not here, that all must pay
Its debt *in full* to time and waste away.
A thousand treasures' endless variety
Will here arrest the traveller's longing eye,
And he will gaze upon this spacious plain
And fancy those beneath the earth long lain
Still living, acting, worshipping once more
In temples where they sacrificed of yore
With reverence deep to gods of wood and stone,
With mystic rites to deities *unknown*.
Invoking Fancy's aid here for awhile,
We may behold the far-extending pile
Of mouldering ruins as they grandly tower
Each above each, mocking as 'twere the power
Of Time their foe : 'tis not a mass of stone
We here behold in wild confusion thrown,
But the vast ruins, far as eye can trace,
Are signal monuments of Egypt's race.

The countless fanes, the obelisks we see,
Are shrines where once, in vain idolatry,
The Pharaohs worshipped, in those alcoves there
Men offered to Osiris fervent prayer.*
Their once glad voices all the fanes around
Far-echoed in their shrines their joyous sound ;
Before those crumbling porticos now raise
No countless throngs their fervent songs of praise,
Nor to these sacred courts do priests draw near
To render sacrifice with hearts sincere.
Oh, that *such* fervour as was wont to fire
Heathens to worship *false* gods, would inspire
Christians to worship Christ revealed and known,
And come with contrite hearts before His throne !
The Zodiac ceilings of the temples prove
Egyptian sages had been taught to love
And study heaven's bright orbits, and to prize
Far beyond earth the treasures of the skies :
They worshipped sun and moon, the day, the night,
But God, who by His word-power infinite
Created sun, moon, stars, earth, sea, and sky,
They worshipped not, slaves to idolatry.
The monolithic statues here displayed
In order regular are still arrayed
In adamantine armour, to oppose
The assaults of Time, the bitterest of foes.

* 'Exclamare litet, populus quod clamat Osiri
    Juvento.'
                    JUVENAL, Sat. viii. 29.

An avenue of sphinxes seems to strive
The lapse of fleeting ages to survive,
Raise heads erect as if old Time to mock,
Who soon to dust will mould each granite
    block.
And close by these, the sepulchre of kings,
Are frail memorials of all mortal things.
They teach the warning lesson that the fate
Of mightiest emperors, their pomp and state,
Their glory, power, like treasures of the earth,
Haste to decay and are of little worth.
Here monarchs lie who never left the field
In brave retreat, who knew not how to yield
When battle raged most furious, men who fought,
As those who from their childhood had been
    taught
To conquer in the struggle or to die,
But never from an enemy to fly:
They fought and o'erthrew nations in their pride,
But soon a mightier victor with swift stride
O'ertook *them*, and their fortitude defied.
Time stole a march on them, Death seized the
    brave,
And soon laid low the conquerors in their grave!
All must have felt, when gazing on a scene
Of greatness or of beauty, there have been
Feelings within the heart words fail to speak,
Thoughts lying deep for language all too weak—

Visions which flit across the Seer's brain
Too high, too noble for an earthly strain.
How shall I picture these ? The task is great,
And powers of the mind inadequate
To tell of these great monuments of stone,
The noblest all the world has ever known.
Here heroes' statues captivate the eye,
Figures colossal rising far on high
Above the palm-tree groves, and here the sight
Of many an old monotholite,
Engraved hieroglyphics, seems to speak
Of æons bygone, and to bid us seek
From these broad pedestals the deeds of those
By whose skilled art these marvellous statues rose!
Here, far around, along the plains extend
Man's resting-places ; here we trace the end
Of those whose works triumphantly could vie
With all the world beside—their fate to die.
We learn from those engravings on the rocks,
Cut out with toil and care on *solid* blocks
Of hardest stone, and here in pride displayed
Beside the bodies mouldering, all that made
Life pleasant to them, all that ever gave
Pleasure to them, naught availed to save
Those princely rulers from the common fate,
Which every son of Adam must await !
They little thought when by affection led
To build such noble mansions for the dead,

That in revolving ages those would be
The abodes of men that love festivity,
And noisy mirth would hold her riot reign
Where the long-buried should in peace remain;
Yet thus it was as Time went onward fast,
To dust he turned the bones men thought would
      last
Through countless ages, and he brushed aside
The signs of splendour, and the marks of pride
Which still lie mouldering here. These tombs
      afford
Dwellings and homes for many an Arab horde;
The glittering mausoleum, where of old
The monarch's body and his crown of gold
With funeral obsequies in state were laid,
Is now the home of the lone shepherd maid;
Now troglodytes these catacombs possess,
And here pass lives in quiet happiness;
Many a veteran Arab here has spent
His span of life, reared children, well content
In this abode—once royal—to live and die,
If thus surrounded by sarcophagi,
With embalmed bodies, haunted with the thought
That once their fathers lay here. They'd been
      taught
To know the gift of happiness and bliss.
Oh! why should we who better know than this

Our fleeting years in discontentment spend,
And life itself too oft with murmurs end ?

     ✳   ✳   ✳   ✳   ✳

Here stands the noblest object of the plain,
On which the eye now looks and rests again,
Lost in astonishment to see where lay
Tanis, who once o'er kings themselves held sway.
Egypt has here her noblest powers of art
Put forth with all her grandeur to impart
Magnificence and glory, and e'en Time
Seems to have favoured well this work sublime,
And in his mercy spared it, for his hand
Has left this rich memorial in the land
Hardly defaced as yet.   On either side
Six columns upward rise in stately pride
Toward the skies, the portico is there,
The inmost sanctuary, the shrine where prayer
From pious hearts was rendered, yet we see
The spot where priest and people bent the knee
In deep devotion, and we rightly feel
True sympathy for those here wont to kneel.
These are the sepulchres where monarchs lay ;
There stand the ruins of the homes where they
Reigned when alive ; those palaces have been
The witnesses of many a royal scene,
These lofty towers which still rise to the sky
Have echoed with the songs of revelry.

The flag of victory has waved afar
When princes came triumphant from the war ;
From these proud heights the prince has often
    scanned
With glist'ning eye the riches of his land ;
Here the seraglio rises in whose tower
The captive maid oft felt the tyrant's power—
Torn from her native shore to be the bride
Of haughty conqueror.   There, too, they have
    died
In bitter agony, whose hearts from grief
In death at length found their long-wished relief.
From these proud turrets oft the madding scream
Has echoed round, and oft the maniac's dream
Of hideous tortures piercing through his brain
Hath made him seek for death, yet seek in
    vain.
There, too, maybe affection's dearest tie
Of mutual love, of holiest chastity,
Hath violated been, the broken heart
Of queen once loved hath felt the bitter smart
Of husband's perfidy, and there has died
In sorrows old the young and lovely bride.

    *   *   *   *   *

The shepherd when he sees the orb of gold
Down sinking in the west, his sheep will fold
Amidst Thebes' ruins, and will gaze afar
With silent reverence on the vesper star

Which evening heralds : 'tis the star which shone
When Homer sang of Thebes.   Homer has gone
To his long sleep—the evening star shines bright
To-night as then, when Homer sang of thee,
O mighty Thebes ! that star thy majesty,
Thy splendour saw and on thy glory smiled,
And o'er thy ruins shed its ray, fair child
Of ancient Egypt, and it still at night
From heaven's height illumes the noble site
Of tottering fabrics which seem yet to rise
As forest trees up to the starlit skies.

    *   *   *   *   *

As years roll on these ruins will decay,
Their fame and splendour pass for aye away.
No vestiges of beauty will be seen,
No trace discovered e'en by glance most keen ;
E'en Hesperus shall lose its brilliancy,
And shine no more with lustre in the sky.
The great Creator who has all things made
Decrees the universe itself shall fade,
That earth and man's works all shall be no more,
That mortals life shall not as heretofore
Be mixed with grief and care, that they should
      die,
And men be happy through eternity.
This shall befall when time has ceased to be,
And death is swallowed up in victory !

LITTLE PRAYERS FROM LITTLE LIPS.

Many years ago I was staying on a visit with others at a sanatorium 7,000 feet above the sea-level, with the wife of a good magistrate and collector, who had been shot through the lung in the Mutiny and miraculously recovered, and never forgot to whom he owed his new life. He was far away in the plains doing his work in the hot weather, but prayer was kept up in his family, and in such a remarkable way as I had never, with a very wide experience, seen before. At early morning family prayers, the mother (as is so often the case in India) led the devotions till she came to the Lord's Prayer—and then she made a marked and striking pause—when a very little daughter, only five years of age, with folded hands and reverent mien, in sweet, childhood's accents, began to say, as I had never heard it said before, the Lord's Prayer, the *elder* members of the family and others following her sentence by sentence. This interesting scene, which deeply impressed me, I have endeavoured to preserve in the following simple lines.

> I HEARD a little girl upraise
>   To God the matin prayer,
> And heavenward lead the note of praise,
>   *Above the pure* mountain air!

‎ ✻   ✻   ✻   ✻   ✻

> I've heard the organ of the choir
>   Peal forth its sweetest strain,
> Floating above till the angel's lyre
>   Seemed to waft it down again.
> I've listened to a white-robed band,
>   Whose well-trained voices chant

God's praises in our fatherland,
  In many a cloistered haunt ;
In fretted nave entranced I've felt
  With psalms and holy song,
And raptured in the chancel knelt
  Amidst the suppliant throng !
But strains heard then did never reach
  So deeply down my heart,
Or to my soul such lessons teach
  As I learnt—from *no skill* or art !—
When a little girl in ' Our Father Prayer '—
  Prayer of all prayers the best—
At her mother's side she had learnt it there,
  Led the prayers of all the rest,
The others following word by word,
  This simple *common* prayer,
*Then needed all it could afford
  To soothe their pain and care.
She knew no trials who prayed it first,
  For in childhood's guileless hours
The impending storm has not yet burst,
  The path is strewn with flowers ;
Yet wise are they who earliest teach
  Their innocents to pray,
For soon the time will come when each
  Needs God's help every day ;

* It was a time of great trial and sorrow.

And as before His throne on high
  Their angels God behold,
He'll hear their prayers acceptably,
  And His succour not withhold !
'Tis wise in childhood's years to train
  The children's hearts to pray,
In after-years they know the gain,
  Who have been taught this way.
When Sorrow lays her chastening hand
  Upon the burdened breast,
Their thoughts will speed to the Better Land,
  And only there seek rest.
When youth and childhood pass away,
  And winter's gloom is near,
When the once fair locks grow thin and gray
  And the leaf is in the sere,
The truths learned at the mother's knee
  Will keep their freshness still,
And the soul with a glowing radiancy
  And peaceful calm o'erfill !
Thus Christians steadfast in prayer's power
  Have the dark valley trod,
And victors in the crucial hour,
  Through Christ found peace with God !
I heard a little girl at prayer
  In the steep Himalayan side,
And these are some thoughts I gathered there
  With a little one for my guide.

MY PHOTOGRAPH BOOK.

The likenesses of friends, children and other relations are
of the highest value to dwellers in a foreign land, and are
again and again reviewed with fond delight.

FACES I loved so deeply, knew so well,
    Come back to me turning these pages o'er;
I long to look on them, I ne'er can tell
    If I shall see them, lovely as of yore—
Not all, for some have passed for aye away,
    From the mixed scenes of this soon fleeting
        life,
And early gone to join in bright array
    Those who have ceased from trouble, trial and
        strife.
One face, the loveliest, arrests my hand,
    I cannot turn from it or pass it by:
She was the fairest of a youthful band,
    And yet almost the first of them to die !
'Tis often thus the sweetest flower which grows
    Smiles all in vain upon the withering blast ;
Its loveliness it neither heeds nor knows,
    But tears it from its roots and hastens past.
Changes are on the face so well defined,
    It shows the traces of the rough world's care,
And looking carefully my eye can find
    That lines of deep and anxious thought are there!

Far from the fatherland we do not feel
   How time rolls on with those we've left behind
As swiftly as with us in woe and weal,
   Changing our friends in figure as in mind !
We oft forget that, in the lapse of years,
   The boy is man we left at home a child,
That she knows now a mother's hopes and fears,
   Who then in all the bloom of girlhood smiled !
That those who prattled at their mother's knee,
   Thoughtless of us when we bid her good-bye,
Are now the pillars of the family,
   And posts of trust and honour occupy.

     *   *   *   *   *

I turn a few more pages and I see
   Some likenesses of little boys and girls,
But these are strangers all unknown to me,
   Though I before have seen such locks and curls ;
Their mother's looks were thus when she was
     young,
   And hers was then as now her daughter's face,
Whilst her dark tresses all so richly hung,
   Though of her beauty hiding not a trace.
In you, her children, I can trace the dead :
   May you to him the vacant place supply
Of the departed one ; and in her stead
   Strive every wish of him to gratify !

     *   *   *   *   *

And other pictures here to me recall,
  Of bygone years a well-remembered scene ;
And gazing fondly on them each and all,
  To memory recall what once has been !
I would not be without my precious book,
  It has for me a pleasure fresh each day ;
I give it every night a lingering look,
  And find it hard sometimes to turn away !
And call it not a weakness ; is it weak,
  Upon our memories the forms to trace
Of those we see no more, hear no more speak,
  Themselves to us revealing face to face ?
Nay, rather 'tis a mark of vigorous mind,
  Of strength of character and manly powers,
To keep our hearts with memories entwined
  Of dearest friends in happy bygone hours !

*   *   *   *   *

EVENING THOUGHTS ON THE DAY OF A CONFIRMATION BY THE LORD BISHOP OF AUCKLAND, NEW ZEALAND.

The Bishop of Auckland was one of my dearest friends, in India, just after the Mutiny, in which he bore an important part as chaplain with Sir Robert Walpole's brigade ; he was appointed to Bareilly, to which station I afterwards succeeded him, and I was appointed to Shajahanpur ; we were forty miles apart, but the distance was not an obstacle to our meeting from time to time. The Bishop came to England, from New Zealand, in 1888, and paid me a visit at the Rectory—we had not met for twenty-five years. The Bishop very kindly held a confirmation, in my little parish, in a church where the oldest inhabitant could not remember a confirmation ever being held before. It was a lovely day in June, and the scene from the beautiful hilltop, on which the church stands, was most striking and impressive. The following lines do but faintly describe it.

THE evening shadows lengthen from above,
  The summer sun sinks gently in the west ;
The nightingales trill forth their notes of love,
  And weary nature seeks her daily rest !
How hallowed seems to me this twilight hour,
  How typical of that foreshadowed time
When mortals, changed by God's Almighty power,
  Shall pass immortal to a happier clime ;
The better Canaan which, the waters past
  Of this tumultuous life, we shall behold,

Gaining our haven long desired at last,
  The sheep returning to the Shepherd's fold.
  *　　　*　　　*　　　*　　　*
O Prince of Peace, I pray Thee, gently guide
  Thy tender lambs along this trying world,
And ever be Thou present at their side,
  Thy banner o'er their guileless hearts unfurl'd.
Teach them in peace the war of truth to wage,
  To know Thy ways their greatest triumph be,
To trace with yearning heart, from sacred page,
  The path which leads to heaven and to Thee.
Give to Thy pledged ones the undying peace
  Which passes understanding, and the love
Which, while they live on earth, shall never cease
  And never fail them in the realms above.
Oh ! take from them the worldling's heart of stone
  And knit their spirits closer unto Thee,
Leading them daily to Thy sacred throne
  As they draw nearer to eternity.
Help them to shun frivolity of mind,
  To ask for seriousness in earnest prayer ;
And each day spent with Thee may evening find
  Their hearts turned heavenward and their
      treasures there.
Train them to live for others, give them light
  To clearly comprehend Thy precious truth ;
Confirm their faith, give them Thy Spirit's light
  To lead them on their path to age from youth.
  *　　　*　　　*　　　*　　　*

IN MEMORIAM, REV. C. H. H.

IN his own churchyard which he loved so well,
   Near by the sanctuary door where, week by
     week,
For twelve years past it was his wont to seek
The presence of his Saviour and forth-tell
To those who worshipp'd with him of His love,
   We laid him down to rest, removed, too soon
   We thought, one sombre Autumn afternoon
'Midst sobs and sighs and unrestrainèd tears
Of friends, relations, and parishioners ;
But not too soon for Him who sums our years
And better knows than we our time for rest.
Resigned to God's decree we have no fears
   For him who ne'er his choir will lead again,
   But find a higher part amidst the angels' strain.

SPRING-TIME.

A FRAGMENT.

THE joyous May has come once more
   With all the flowers she used to bring,
   And songsters who as gaily sing
As they were wont in springs of yore.

It seems not like the Mays to me
To which my heart would fondly cling,
Which still live in my memory.
Blest days of boyhood's innocence,
When cowslip, daisy, and bluebell
Had charms for me! ye've fled far hence,
And much with you that I loved well.

THE ISLE OF LIGHT.

This poem was written by me just after my ordination, in
1857, when our hearts were saddened by the fearful tidings
which came from India, to which allusion is made in the
opening lines. When chaplain of Darjeeling, in 1863, I
sent it to *Chesson and Woodhall's Miscellany*, at Bombay,
in which periodical it appeared, and was very favourably
reviewed by an indulgent Indian press.

I.

My heart was aching, saddened by the tales
Of war and tumult which from India came
In those dark days when Britain's sons were
    slain,
And wives and daughters died heroic deaths!
I did not sleep, and yet I seemed to dream;
It hardly yet was night; the sun, though low,
Was shining bright with western splendour red;
It was the even time, the hour of peace,

And day declined in autumn quietude,
While o'er the landscape lengthening shadows fell.

      *   *   *   *   *

I seemed to wander thro' a forest wild,
A tangled jungle dense with towering trees,
Now shedding teardrops o'er the dying year;
A soughing wind their branches gently waved,
And gleams of fading sunlight flashing by
Formed myriad brilliant circles, rainbow-bright.
A stream of crystal waters, silver-tinged,
Meandered thro' the thicket ; on each bank
Grew forest flowers of various hues and tints,
Their drooping petals moist with evening dew ;
It was a lovely stream, its wavelets seemed
Clearer than those of earthly rills to me ;
The setting sun, the rising moon shone full
Upon it now and traced a glistening path
As far as I could gaze ; such have I seen
When sailing on the sea at sunset hour,
A bright track leading to some Arab isle.
By some all-powerful spell I seemed led on,
I could not linger nor my steps retrace,
But onward wandered, ever musing, where
The smoothly flowing stream my steps would lead.
I reck'd no danger from those furious beasts
Which Indian jungles haunt and men destroy ;
So happy in the present, I forgot
My bygone cares, nor thought of coming ills ;

All power of thinking of what yet might be
Was taken from me; an entrancing joy,
Soothing anxiety and undefinable,
O'erspread my spirit and my inmost soul
With its sweet influence; thus I forgot
The world, its troubles and widespread distress.
What blest oblivion! what surpassing bliss!
To lull to sleep for only one short hour
The stern and bitter cares of toiling life,
To lose in sweet forgetfulness the thoughts
Sadly entwined around the mourning heart,
Reviving scenes of bloodshed, sorrow, woe!
What happiness to be at rest awhile
Amidst the busy scenes of active life;
In solitary mood to contemplate
The various deeds and actions of mankind;
Taking no part in these, but viewing all
As angels might who see them from above!
Asking the end, the object of all works
Which eager men assiduously perform,
Seeking the reason of incessant toil,
The cause and need of ever-labouring hands!
Oh! how I feel for those hard slaving ones
Who eat the bread of care and late take rest,
Too little loved, too seldom honoured here,
And trusting ever their best Friend above!
Along the path I trod I saw no serf,
No hand as yet luxuriant Nature's growth

Had checked, a wilderness around,
Untrod by human step, untill'd, unknown,
Dank, wild, and gloomy; yet my path was light,
And as I onward sped it brighter grew;
A distant way I wandered, and the stream
A mighty river, Ganges-like, became,
Changing its course and issuing thro' the wood,
Meandered by a wide and fertile vale.
It was a valley lit with rays of light,
Dazzling beyond the splendour of the sun.
The trees beside the waters in full bloom
Bore leaves like emeralds, the flowers shone
As glistening diamonds on the river's bank;
The stream itself was clear as crystal glass,
Its gentle wavelets softly murmured by,
And on their quiet surface I beheld
A snow-white sail fast fading to the west.
I wondered for what country it was bound,
And how its crew could meet the dazzling glare
Which now suffused and hid their sail from me.
Here was I terror-struck, and dared not move
Further along this bright mysterious path.
I shuddered when I thought how over-bold,
How rash I was to venture on this way,
And felt I was unworthy to pursue
The pathway thro' the valley; there I thought
The splendour and the glory would eclipse
My feeble vision, and I seemed to think

I was not clad in raiment meet to join
With those bright beings who might enter there.
Deeply and sadly grieved I half resolved
My footsteps to retrace; when, looking back,
I saw the path which led me was no more—
No track was visible, no foothold there.
Backward I could not, forward I dared not, move,
And, thus confounded, seemed for ever lost;
Deeply I grieved and trembled to advance
To the bright realms beyond my ravished sight.
While thus perplexed there fell upon my ear
A voice both sweet and kind, yet so unlike
The voice of man, that I, tho' overjoyed
To feel that one however strange was near,
Trembled at listening to the words it spoke:
'This is the way, and in it you shall walk,
When aught shall tempt you to the right or left.
These are the words of Him who is *the Truth*,
Strait is the gate and narrow is the way.'
Then nearer came the voice, and I knew well
Some noble being stood before my eyes;
I felt as those of old who, when they saw
The glistening face of him who led them through
The wild and burning Wilderness of Sin,
That I must not behold his countenance,
When lo! he nearer came and thus he spoke:
'O wanderer, weep not nor cast down thine eyes,
Thou mayest enter yonder radiant land,

And I will be thy guide.   Come follow me.'
Cheered by his voice I ventured to behold
The form of him who spoke ; a spirit seemed
To move beside me from some better world.
His face shone brighter than the mid-day sun,
His raiment, white and glistening, fell in folds,
Encircling gracefully his noble mien
And yet impeded not his fleeting step.
He did not seem to walk, but glide along,
Like the swift summer bird whose taper wing
The air divides and leaves no trace behind.
I saw him cross a bridge whose arches spanned
The river's silver waters ; it was built
With sardius, chrysolite and beryl stones,
Its arches turned with sapphires, glancing light.
Amazed at all I saw, afraid to speak,
In silence crossed, following close my guide.
We now had entered on another shore,
The valley traversed I before had seen ;
And deemed myself unworthy to be there !
Fairer and richer than Thessalian glades,
Adorned with lovelier flowers than grew of old
In Tempe's cultured groves and flower-clad dells.
Innumerable plants, none could reveal
Their various names ; as well essay
To reckon all the stars or calculate
The countless hosts of heaven.   Some I knew,
The rose of Sharon *here* was in full bloom,

And *there* I saw it, bursting from its buds.
There seemed no blasts of winter raging here,
But ever summer time; no faded flower,
Nor one imperfect blossom could I trace,
Amongst the myriad lilies; these I knew,
They were familiar all, and yet so changed,
As if no earthly sun had given them life.
These, I reflected, toil not, do not spin,
And yet royal monarch on ancestral throne,
Tho' clad in purple robes, is not arrayed
Like one of these sweet unpretending flowers.
Oh! how I longed to lay me down in rest
Amidst the groves of this sequestered vale;
How my heart beat to ask my unknown guide
What name was his and from what land he came,
Where I had wandered and whence issued forth
The strains of heaven-born music, which I heard
Floating around me like the hum of bees,
Or busy insects on a summer's day—
Anon resembling the full-chorused chants
Of nature's aviary in joyous May!
And my desire was granted; he divined
Or seemed to fathom all my inmost soul,
And lingering by me spake these wondrous words:
'Who would not, wanderer, long like thee to rest
Beneath these towering cedars, and repose
For ever in this island of the blest?
This is a happy land, the songs thou hearest

Cease never here ; anon shalt thou behold
Those who have charmed thee with their soothing
    strains.
But rest awhile, as thou dost wish ; then ask
Whate'er thou wilt and I will not withhold
All that is meet for mortal frail to know.'
' May I then ask,' said I, ' thy history ?
Much that is dark to me will then be clear.'
' Thou may'st,' said he ; ' I am *the Penitent.*
I did not always wear these shining robes,
Made white for aye, the generous gift
Of Him I freely serve but once disowned.
In stranger garb I mingled among men,
For I have worn (with grief and shame I own)
The prisoner's chains and malefactor's badge.
I lived a life of madness, folly, sin,
From wrong to deepest crime I madly rushed,
First God forgot, blasphemed, then cruelly robb'd,
At length my wretched hands imbued in blood,
And 'gainst the innocent my dagger raised ;
Then, branded with the murderer's black badge,
They led me forth to die a felon's death.
My guilty conscience owned my sentence just,
Tho' I denied my guilt, afraid to die.
'Twas all in vain ; triumphant justice doomed
Another and myself to die ; but there was One
With us dragged cruelly to the place of skulls,
Whom envious despots suffered not to live.

He was most meek, more lowly than the sons
Of men earth-born ; but none so foully mocked,
Despitefully entreated, and traduced,
As the most innocent and pure in heart,
Bearing His weight of woe and heeding not
The jeers and scoffs of roughest soldiery.
He gently passed where reverent women wept,
And daughters of the city wailed his fate.
The gibes He answered not, but like a lamb,
Unconscious of its end to slaughter led,
He suffered men to drag Him to the spot,
Where earth's off-scouring, wicked, crime-dyed
     men
Passed thro' a fiery trial, in torture racked,
Outbreathed their souls in miserable death—
Here we were *rightly*, He *unjustly*, fixed
On cruel crosses one on either side,
But He was in the midst ; how little thought
The foes who bound us that by merest chance
Betwixt us twain His place was well assigned !
Thus ever stood He, God be praised ! still stands,
The only Mediator-Advocate,
The innocent between the guilty placed.
Our sufferings were great, His heavier still,
The sweat of agony from His pierced brow
Kept issuing forth in heavy drops of blood.
The travail of His soul no voice, no tongue,
Has ever yet described, or can express.

Far more than Man he suffered, for He bore
The weight of the world's sins; His wounded frame
Was more than ours bemarred. His thirst
     intense
By no friend's hand was slaked; a cooling draught
From Cedron's gurgling brook was all He wished—
They gave Him gall and vinegar instead.
And, more than this, they foully struck His face,
Scoffing derisively they wagged their heads.
In mock humiliation, bowing down,
Paid empty homage to their dying King.
I cannot tell thee all the grief I felt,
(For here we scarce remember sorrow's hours),
When I beheld my fellow-suffering thief
Join in reviling this most righteous Man.
I thus indignantly met his rebuke :
" What! dost not *thou* fear God, seeing that you,
In condemnation stand more just than He ?
And we indeed most rightly do receive
The sentence of our deeds, while this good Man
Hath never done amiss. Remember me,
Good Lord, in that blest day when Thou
Dost enter in Thy kingdom." Turning round,
And bending on me His soul-melting look,
He spoke these few consolatory words :
" In truth I say to thee, With Me to-day
E'en thou shalt be in Paradise." What joy
Thrilled thro' my soul! I had not heard

One loving word for many a long-passed year
Addressed *to me;* my life began with those
Who lisped in oaths and curses, but in love
A word they breathed not.　Like sunshine upon
　　　snow
That voice fell on my heart, till then of adamant.
It soon dissolved, it beat with gratitude
And glowing love to Him who ever cheers
Returning sinners with a heavenly smile.
I turned to thank Him, then my eye meet His;
When there shall be eternity no more
That gentle, loving look I shall forget—
But not till then.　All heaven seemed to shine
Upon that bleeding face.　I scarce had heard
A heaven there was above; I saw it *there,*
Reflected clear as, on some river's wave
In winter's night, you see the twinkling stars,
Not really as they are yet shadowed forth.
Thus I enjoyed a *shadow* of the gift
I was to realize *to-day,* and I could trace
In that brief glance upon His countenance
Faith, hope, and love; and I could *trust*
That voice I heard and He who spoke the words.
With Him I knew that happy I should pass
The bitterness of death my soul must taste.
Led by His hand, fearless I should surmount
The cross's agonies; and triumphing,
Amidst the songs of angels joying o'er ME,

" Enter with Him the paradise of God."
If thou art weary, rest thee here in peace ;
Then further mysteries thou shalt perceive.'

II.

He spake, and vanished quickly from my ken,
Like some bright dream, half finished,
The happy sleeper summons back in vain
To hear its end.   Thus I in solitude
Surveyed more closely those enchanted scenes
I had admired when listening to the words
My guide was uttering ; now I laid me down
Beside the watercourses, downward flowing
From mountain springs above, and thought of those
Which bards of Greece and Rome had sweetly
        hymned,
Of their Castalia mused, and called to mind
The glassy, clear Bandusia, and I knew
That these, tho' worshipped by Apollo's sons,
Whose fame survives as yet in lyric strains,
Could not compare with those before my eyes.
A fountain clear of living waters this,
And they who from its sources drew one draught
Should never thirst again ; and, more than this,
A healing power, virtue miraculous,
Like some Siloam's pool, this stream possessed ;
And those who laved in it their halting limbs

Or body paralyzed were straight made whole.
When they emerged they other beings seemed,
In image and in nature new-created,
Cleansed from all stains and wholly purified.
Here I beheld a sight most marvellous—
The beasts of prey, which in the jungle roar
And one another kill and then devour,
Did not their enemies destroy or hurt ;
The timid lamb beside the ravening wolf
Lay sleeping peacefully, nor sought her dam
To shield her from a foe ; the dappled fawn
Dreaded not here the cheetah's certain spring—
Joined in their frisky games each friends with
    each,
While on the same green bank their mothers fed.
What unseen power their savage natures changed ?
What more than human influence could com-
    mand
Passive obedience from the untamed beasts ?
No power but one—the Infinite Divine.
I mused on this strange scene, half wondering
If *men* would thus grow wiser and renounce
Their evil passions, peace-destroying strife,
Or reap the fruits of bitter enmity.
As long as man was man, would nations learn,
Though differing in language, customs, laws,
To join in union, and with one accord
Profess a common faith, adore one only God ?

Would man in every climate 'neath the sun,
Where'er he lived, a brother's greeting find ;
And meet not through the world an open foe,
Or, worse than all, a false, insidious friend ?
Will our corrupted natures be renewed
By some bright spirit's renovating breath,
So that the words by which we now describe
All that is sinful, evil, or depraved
Shall be to those who hear them language dead ?
Oh, longed-for time! then earth will not be earth,
But heaven descended ; for what is heaven to us
But earth devoid of sin and its results ?
Oh, longed-for hour ! the universal reign
Of happiness and peace ; no golden age,
No fabled æon, when the gods descend
From heaven to usurp the place of men ;
But that blest time when all men shall be free,
Enjoying social freedom, and no slave
To base pursuits or evil tempter's power.
'Tis true we're fallen beings, fallen far,
And maybe falling yet—still, not bereft
Of power and capacity ; of pinions strong,
Exerting faith in which we may arise
Higher immeasurably than we ever fell
If never so degraded.   Happy they
Who such a metamorphosis behold
In human creatures !   Can such ever be ?
I heard, or seemed to hear, a voice reply

In answer to my queries.   Looking round,
Close by my side, approaching noiselessly,
Another spiritual being I beheld;
He much resembled him who led me first
Into this happy isle, but elder seemed,
And yet, not old, so bright his countenance.
I looked on him with awe, and listened still
While thus he spoke: 'Thou wonderest, dear friend,
If fallen man in nature can be changed;
If the depraved, corrupted, destitute,
Tainted with crime, contaminating sin,
Afflicted with base passions, uncontrolled
By conscience or by reason; if men, cursed
With evil dispositions such as those
Whom Satan bound with iron fetters once,
Or whose sad spirits, blackened and defiled
With envious purpose or impure desires,
Conceive and perpetrate the schemes of hell;
If these and such as these can be reformed,
As to resemble innocents new-born?
Is this the problem which perplexed thy mind?'
I answered him: 'Thou hast divined my thoughts.
And may I ask if thou hast power to solve
These theories too arduous for me?'
Thus he: ' I can, and am myself a proof
Of all that thou wouldst know.   I will unfold
The story of my life; mark well its course,
And learn how, from a worthless, fallen man,

A glad and happy being I became.
In life's springtime I left my father's home ;
A younger son, a wild and thoughtless youth,
I took my journey to a foreign land,
Indulging there in every vain excess,
In gross licentiousness I squandered
All the inheritance which fell to me.
I had exhausted every kind of joy—
Sensual, earthly, devilish.   Then I felt
The pangs of hunger ; delicately nursed,
And cradled in the lap of luxury,
I could not labour ; glad was I to fill
My belly with the husks the swine did eat,
While those dear friends who joined my revelry,
Or shared the feasts *my* bounty freely gave,
No longer courted my companionship,
Or gave a single crumb to drive away
Starvation's famined phantom from my sight.
This is the worldling's dogma ; can he gain
Pleasure or self-aggrandisements from thee,
No one so friendly, none so loves thee then.
But lose thy power, thy influence or wealth ;
Thy once warm friend now coldly slinks away,
And, like some skulking cur from poor man's cot,
Seeks the lord's kitchen and the scullion's meal.'
'Too true,' I said ; 'but how didst thou escape
Thy close impending fate and dreadful death ?'
'Ah ! friend,' said he, 'I came unto myself ;

Myself till *then* I never truly knew.
And what a vile, ungrateful wretch was I !
What untold agony, what bitter tears,
Had I caused *him* who watched me from the
    hours
Of prattling childhood with a father's care !
What grief to *her* who gently me up-trained
From earliest infancy !   How cruelly
Requited I a dearest mother's love !
This all flashed on me now, as we behold,
In some dark thunderstorm, the forkèd light
Discover in an instant objects wrapt
In black obscurity ; so I descried
In one brief second hideous and black spots
On my past life.   Thus I came to myself.
Oh, what a crushed and wasted wreck I felt !
Methought some thick and gloomy blight had
    spread
A life-destroying poison thro' my soul.
And then I sadly wept tears, bitter tears,
Of penitence and sorrow from my heart.
My thoughts reverting to my father's house,
I well remembered many menials there
Had food in plenty, while my pallid cheeks
Each day became more hollow, my frail frame
Daily declined and I drew nigh to death ;
A living man, I seemed not half alive.
Then I resolved I homeward would return,

And seek once more the roof I had foresworn;
Confess my base ingratitude and own
My deep-dyed sins, my evil purposes,
And falling on my face, heart-broken, sad,
Entreat my father's pardon and implore
His free forgiveness for my evil ways.
When I drew near our homestead I beheld
The good old man advance toward his son;
Some unknown messenger the tidings bore
Of his lost one's return.   I eager ran
To throw my arms around him, and confessed
I was unworthy to be called his son.
His tears with mine were mingled; his of joy
And mine of sorrow—rain with sunshine mixed,
As 'tis in spring-time—I who ne'er had felt
The love a son *should* to his father bear,
The almost holy reverence and regard
Due from a youth to one whose silver hairs
Marked him entitled to a Nestor's claim
To honour and obedience from his child.
I, thoughtless, careless, little understood
A parent's fondness or a father's love
For one who is of all the youngest born !
How oft the deep-fixed springs of earnest love
Had welled up from his heart whene'er he thought
In lonely hours of his lost, wandering boy !
In many a sleepless hour his o'erwrought mind
Pictured his erring-one, 'midst scenes of woe,

Surrounded by vile comrades steeped in crime,
Enticing, tempting, leading far astray
Their younger dupe, whose all too pliant will,
Led captive at their pleasure, led him on
From sin to sin, till he at length became
A lost, depraved, and ruined prodigal !
Or, when he slept, how oft in dreams appeared
The son upbraiding the indulgent hand
Which curbed not in his youth his strong self-will,
Nor checked his froward pride! Thus, undeserved,
Himself he would condemn for negligence;
But now, when locked again in his embrace,
I realized the sorrow I had caused
My loving parent, and myself reproached
With blighting his last days and bringing down
His hoary head with sorrow to the grave.
He would not hearken to my self-rebukes,
Nor leave me lying prostrate at his feet ;
He was my father yet, and I his son.
He gently raised me up, and, kissing me,
Led me once more beneath his happy roof.
Nor was this all, nor ended here his love :
His lost one was restored, his dead alive ;
He would not see his son in hireling's garb,
But clothed me in light raiment ; on my hand
He placed a costly ring; the fatted calf
Was straightway killed, the welcome feast out-
     spread,

Old friends were called to greet me, young ones
　　　joined
The happy circle, young and old alike
Welcomed with joy the prodigal's return.'
' Did you forsake your home again ?' I asked.
' No, not for years, and then I could not stay ;
The hour was come—home was no longer home.
With gentle hand I closed my father's eyes,
I watched him tenderly as mother would
Her dying child ; no want, no wish
I left unsatisfied ; soon my hour came
To follow him, how changed I have described.
You see me bright and happy, the reward
Of deep repentance and a contrite heart.
This lesson learn, then, from my history :
Evil avoid, God honour and obey.'

III.

Thus ended, leaving me to ponder
O'er his weird history, his voice refreshed
My wearied soul ; in pensive mood I roamed
Further along the valley, and beneath
Lebanon's cedars' shade I trod a path
Which led to brighter regions still, and heard
The harmonious strains of thousand voices sweet
In unison combined, and there I saw
An aviary of songsters ; clearer far

Than melancholy Philomel they sang
Their joyous notes ; there is no *evening* song,
For there is no night there, nor e'en the twilight
     hour.
No setting sun or dark uprising clouds
Foretold a coming night or boisterous storm ;
Here all was light, and as I onward moved,
More perfect brilliancy, more perfect peace
Was all around diffused : I ne'er had felt
Tranquillity till now ; my enraptured soul
Experienced more than language can define.
Like others, I had read the thoughtful works
Of old and new philosophers, had explored
Their varied notions of man's happiness.
But, oh ! how infinitely wisest sage,
Profoundest theorist and loftiest bard
Had failed to realize that perfect peace
Which now was mine ; I fondly wished
My dearest friends with me for one short hour
To share the joy that I now realized
What happiness is theirs who, in this world,
In frivolous excitement spend their days
Without a thought and scarce a wish beyond ?
Who never know an hour of peaceful rest ;
Their days of rest, Sabbaths unhallowèd
Which should be holy but polluted are
Either by earthly work or schemes conceived
To be enacted in the coming week !

How much of peace they lose could they have
    felt
My present sweet retirement and repose !
The heaped-up treasures of their busiest years
To purchase such a gem they would have given.
I could not comprehend why such sweet peace
More than elsewhere should here triumphant reign
Through all the fertile valley ; soon I heard
The problem troubling then my mind made clear.
I now had reached a place where two ways met,
And, doubting with myself which track to choose,
I looked around me, when, to my surprise,
One, beautiful as those I saw before,
Once more appeared in view ; he seemed at rest,
Yet not asleep ; his clear blue eyes met mine.
Perplexed and wondering he on me smiled
Sweeter than mother on her sleeping babe,
And then without an effort, undisturbed
By my abrupt appearance gently spake :
' Thou seemst,' said he, ' to have lost thy way.'
Then I : ' Yes, lost am I, and know not whither
    now
My footsteps should be turned, nor can I tell
Where I have wandered or this country's name.'
Then he to me : ' It would be passing strange
If thou couldst understand or comprehend
The deep mysterious secrets of this land.
These regions, more than any known to you,

Are the abodes of happiness and peace ;
The spirits who abide here interweave
A chain of love which ne'er can be dissolved ;
Here it is fastened, but continuèd
By reverent hands to yet another clime,
And there it ends.   I may not lead thee there.
Some holier One may guide thee if thy faith
Firmly holds fast His hand until the end.
I see, you long to know how I came here,
And by what title I am named and live.'
Then thus I answered : 'Thou hast divined the
        thoughts
Which even now are passing through my mind.'
' Then listen,' he responded.   ' Long ago—
So many years it seems, I scarce know when,
So many æons have I spent since then
Of heaven-sent joy—I wore the beggar's garb,
The tattered rags of hated poverty ;
My wasted frame half-clad, they called me then
A beggar and a vagrant ; I was shunned
By woman, man, and child ; my poverty
A crime was deemed, as if I had been God
To overrule the ruthless hand of Death
Which seized my father, or could have prolonged
A loving mother's life who early slept
That sleep the lot of man ; an orphan boy,
Alone, unfriended in a cruel world,
And this not all my woe, I was infirm,

My body paralyzed while yet a child,
And as I older grew I scarce could drag
My aching limbs along from house to house,
From town to town ; for years I wanderèd
And laid not down my weary head at night
On softened pillow, but my couch I sought
On the wild desert or the lonely wold.
Mine not to know the sweet, the holy charm
The blessed words " my home " to some suggest ;
No living hand pressed mine, no dear one's heart
To mine responsive beat ; no voices kind
Of sisters and of brothers sweetly mixed
Gently fell on my ears ; no joyous looks
Beaming with love or fond affection's smile
Met me returning home.   Those who know
The sweet endearing comfort of a home,
Affinities existing in the souls
Of those who form a happy family,
Closely knit fast by links of brotherhood,
The happy interchange of family thoughts
Experienced when long-parted ones re-meet,
Know not the loneness of a wanderer's life ;
He looks on different faces every day,
But claims with none a kin ; they look on him,
Some with aversion, others pitying,
But all as if they felt slight interest
Or sympathy for him ; could they but scan
The story of his life, reveal one page

Of his untold misfortunes, they would learn
Man's chequered fate, the mutability
Of all things mundane; they would, maybe, reflect
That, though their lot is now an envied one,
The fakir,* crouching prostrate at their door,
May rise to their high place, they to *his* fall.
Such changes there have been, will be again.
How little ken the opulent of earth
The poor man's hardships or his bitter trials,
His great capacity for joy; yet these
Were destined in this life to be his lot.
There are who think there is a wide gulf fixed
Between the rich and poor; the unrefined,
Uncultivated masses they suppose
Shaped of other clay and formed from dust
Less rare and fine than that of their own mould;
They do not think that those of meaner form
Possess the spirit, bright intelligence,
Or varied talents God has given *them*.
Delusive thoughts! For all these precious gifts
To man are given by one impartial hand.
Some favoured with advantage others lack
Exhibit to the world their brilliant parts;
These can display the genius which lies hid
In minds untrained yet still existing there.
There is no difference, save conventional,
Between the high and low; the same good God

* Beggar in India.

Created all in His similitude,
And breathed into their souls *like* breath of life.
Why, then, was I an outcast ?—'twas God's will.
Why borne about from house to house to crave
The crumbs which from the lordly tables fell,
I will make known and thus complete my tale.
Mine *was* a miserable life and full of pain;
Sometimes I rested by the temple gate
Which men called beautiful, and justly called.
With jewels and pearls inlaid, it brightly flashed,
As of the Taj Mahal* on Jumna's bank ;
And at the hours of prayer 'twas beautiful
To see the crowds press in to worship God ;
Day after day they came by families,
Fathers and mothers led their children here
To join the throngs of reverent worshippers;
And when these happy groups, joined hand in hand,
Passed by me through the court my loneliness
I felt acutely ; and then I could bless
Those children innocent, whose tiny hands
Placed in the poor man's bag their willing doles.
At other times I dragged me to the porch
Of one well known for his magnificence
And gorgeous luxury, in purple royal,
And finely-woven linen, Tyrian-dyed,
He fed most sumptuously ; I *without* could see
The daily banquet spread, and, starving, heard

* Tomb at Agra in India.

The servants staggering under loads of meat
Wherewith to deck the table of their lord.
He, wretched man (truly a miser he),
Thought little of the suppliant at his gate ;
His boon companions entering deigned not look
With pity or compassion on my sores.
And, when the feast was o'er, passed out again,
And, flushed with wine, him whom they spurned
        before
Now mocked and cursed with awful devilry.
Though foully used I was not friendless left,
For, lo ! the dogs, more human far than they,
Sagacious creatures who would quickly rend
From limb to limb a villain or a knave,
By instinct licked the honest beggar's sores.
Mine *was a life of woe ;* see my reward,
And learn from me how deals a righteous God
With all His creatures.   The just Father loves.
You have divined my name, 'tis Lazarus,
And Abraham's bosom is this holy place.
You see how changed my lot, and can explain
The changeless law and rule of Providence.
If e'er perplexed by His mysterious acts,
When at a loss to comprehend His ways,
When pondering why some creatures groan with
        pain,
Or secret sorrows breaking down their hearts,
And dragging on a seeming woeful life

Whilst others live in sunshine all their days,
Without one cloud of sadness on their path ;
Seek not to disentangle mysteries,
Deep as are these, but ever exercise
A steady faith in God.   Remember, He
Has told us His best name of all is " Love."
That He does all things well for those He loves,
And though much to thy sight seems passing
        strange,
To *you* unjust, or contrary to right,
Reflect ! when He comes, justice will be done
To all by Him who is our righteous Judge.'

IV.

Thus ending he departed, and I heard
The sound of holy voices floating down
The valley's gentle slopes.   As on they came,
Nearer and nearer, the words I understood
They sweetly sung ; then once more lost the strain,
As I have heard on some bleak wintry day,
When village bells ring out their welcome peals,
What time the day draws near of Jesu's birth ;
From many towers sweet music, pealing forth,
Spreads over hill and dale, commingling now
In perfect harmony and erst recedes,
As if borne back by some rough wave of wind,
And only faintly caught by listening ear.
'Twas thus I heard the strain of this new song

The unknown voices sang : ' Worthy the Lamb—
The spotless Lamb—who died for us,' they cry.
Clearer and clearer yet these voices sound,
Nearer the music comes ; now I behold
The holy band approach, all children they
Whose lips with words of guile were never stained,
Whose feet in crooked paths had never trod,
Whose minds had harbour found for no ill
    thought,
Whose hearts were ne'er corrupt with sinful lust ;
Pure, holy, undefiled.   How beautiful!
What holy beings these !   And such as these
Were they who sang Hosannahs to our Lord,
Who graced His march triumphant, from whose
    mouths
Praise is perfected ; well I understood
Those words of Him who spake as never man :
' Of such is Heaven's Kingdom,' and as such
Must all be who would hope to enter there.
They, too, were clothed in robes of spotless white,
A crown of gold, enriched with sparkling gems,
Their brows encircled like a wreath of flowers ;
Their tuneful harps they carried in their hands,
And when one swept the chords the others seemed
By sympathetic love to do the same.
Then, as the sound of many waters, flowed
The streams of music which my soul entranced.
Amazed and lost, I would have given worlds

To join their song, but this my voice refused.
My lips were moveless and the song was new,
By me not comprehended ; 'twas too deep
For human utterance, above mortals' ken.
The throng sped onward, and I strove to grasp
And treasure up their notes : the trial failed.
I then essayed to follow the bright throng :
The attempt was vain, they soon to sight were lost,
While I, spellbound and wondering, upward gazed.
No one I deemed had witnessed my surprise,
Or understood my thoughts I then supposed
The vision I in solitude had seen.
So perfectly absorbed, I noticed not
A bright one at my side ; I saw her now
Advancing to my side, as lovely she
As those I'd seen before, or lovelier,
For all were glorious here, and each I saw
Seemed to outshine the last in excellence.
Her name I asked, and ' Mary ' she replied.
Her history she told me, how of yore,
With tears of sorrow, she had laved the feet
Of One despised, rejected by mankind.
How He in love and sweet compassion looked
On her who felt for Him ; and how He spoke
Words sweeter far than honey to her soul—
How He forgave her sins ! those sins, how sad !
Spread o'er a lifetime.   What a harrowing tale
Did she to me reveal!   She was forgiven.

Oh ! happiness; how peacefully she passed
Her after-life devoted to her Lord.
Hers was a penitent and contrite heart.
She told me of repentance, sighs and tears,
Of soul bowed down with suffering for the past
But still buoyed up with hope ; the word despair
Her lips had uttered ne'er.   There was no need
For sinners to despond, the vilest man
Might seek forgiveness at His feet where she
Had poured her grief, and find his *perfect peace*.
Her face as sunbeams shone when she disclosed
The holy influence which Jesu's words
Breathed on her breast, forgiving all her crime.
With animated eloquence she spoke ;
Language transcending all I'd heard before
Flowed from her lips in an unbroken stream,
Of which my spirit never weary grew.
It oft had been my lot to feel a charm,
Which seemed as magic spell my soul to bind,
When listening to some gifted orator.
A power mysterious.   What a charmer he
Who can enchain the minds of listening throngs
As he descants upon some genial theme,
Employing language springing, as it were,
Like a clear rill, spontaneous from his heart ;
Most exquisitely chosen to describe,
As 'twere, without an effort, all his mind !
Now o'er my soul some such enthralling power

This holy one possess'd. From her I learnt,
To my request responsive, who were those
Who harped upon their strings the strains I heard :
' For those sweet babes, those holy innocents,
Had many a mother wept a woman's tears ;
And hands, bloodstained, to carry out
The sinful purpose of a cruel king,
Had from their mothers' bosoms wildly snatched
These helpless ones ; their swords had done the
        rest,
And early driven them to the infant's grave.
But mothers,' she continued, ' while they weep
For loss of such as they, should lay to heart
That little ones when taken from their sight
Are mercifully removed from ill to come.
Rough winds bear off the buds as well as flowers ;
For buds may flourish in God's Paradise
As do the full-formed flowers ; angels bright
Were children once, and harmless infants now
From innocency pass unstained to heaven.
You saw yon group of white-robed ones, and wept
When I made known to you their bitter fate.
Grieve not for these, behold their present joy,
A joy which man can never wrest from them ;
Nor care nor earthly sorrow marred their brows ;
No disappointment such as falls to us,
No tears for loved ones gone bedewed their cheeks,
No words of passion issued from their mouths,

No evil thoughts conceived ; pure, undefiled,
To heaven from earth they passed. For them
    mourn not.
I spoke to you of sorrow-stricken ones,
Of men whose hearts would well-nigh break when
    they
In sad old age reviewed their vanished lives,
And as they scann'd their chequered pages o'er
Would soon discover many a darkling blot
That they would fain erase ; grave, hideous sins
Committed thoughtlessly, bitterly recalled ;
They will look back on days and years long gone,
Misspent in folly and base wickedness,
And they will utterance give to words of grief,
Sad notes of penitence, regret, remorse.
These—what a contrast ! They such words knew
    not—
To them no meaning bring ; their little life
Was one unclouded day of childhood's joy.
For these mourn not, and grieve not at the thought
That millions yet will join this happy band.'
She, ceasing, glided gently from my sight ;
I, musing, followed, wondering in my heart
What next I would behold, when suddenly
The village bells rang out the vesper chime ;
Their sound my dream dispelled, and worshippers
In various groups of old and young combined,
Pensive and thoughtful, to the house of God

Their footsteps bent ; not spirits these but men.
Still men, who, by God's grace, shall angels be.
And musing thus I joined the pious throng,
And offered up with them our evensong.

A MIDNIGHT VISIT TO A STROLLING VAN.

THE jubilee clock in the gray church tower
Was slowly striking the midnight hour,
So cloudy the night, no silvery sheen
Of moonbeams fell light o'er the fields green,
And so still was the hour, that the shriek of the owl
Seemed loud on the hill as the jackal's wild howl,
As a messenger hurried with eager feet
Swiftly along the still village street,
To the home of the lady up at the hall,
The friend, when in need, of the villagers all,
Entreating her ladyship, without delay,
To visit a poor woman, passing away,
As they thought ; and the lady, though seeking
          her rest,
E'er *awake* to the cry of the sad or distrest,
The messenger following, came to the scene
Where the woman was lying in a van on the green.
'Twas the village feast-day and the strollers were
          there

Who wander about from race and to fair—
A strange folk are they, some bad and some good,
Who precariously gain in this way their food.
When the men drink and lie idle, alas! the poor
      wives
Know little of comfort or peace in their lives;
And thus 'twas with her whose tale we relate,
Who implored the good lady to pity her fate.
Nor in vain, for a feeling of sympathy true
Touched her heart when of grief or sorrow she knew.
She climbed up the steps and entered the door
Of the van, and espied, in a bed on the floor,
By a dip dimly burning, the starving young wife,
Worn down with pain, hard gasping for life.
The experienced lady who by her side knelt
The comfort she needed instinctively felt,
And on good impulse acting, was quick to obtain
The nourishment needed the life to sustain.
A certificate, too, for the infirmary near
Was given and used, as was known the next year;
And, how strange is the story, both woman and
      man
Disappeared the next morn, and no trace of the van
On the green could be seen. And a year rolled
      away,
Till once more came round the village feast-day;
When, as the good lady was passing along,
And mingling freely amongst the glad throng,

Here and there speaking kindly to young and to
  old,
As was her wont, for to none was she cold,
A young woman, looking so cheerful and gay,
A low curtsey made as she passed on her way.
To the lady a stranger, ' Don't you know me ?' she
  said ;
' I'm the woman they thought that day would be
  dead,
When your ladyship came in the dead of the night
And cheered my sad heart like an angel of light.
May God of His goodness every day bless
The good lady who helps the poor in distress.'

IN MEMORIAM, M. M. R. H.

DIED ÆTAT. FIFTEEN YEARS, ELEVEN MONTHS.

ONLY an orphan girl—
  Fatherless, motherless she—
Here, far from the noise and busy whirl
  Of the world, sleeps peacefully.

Away from cities and towns,
  O'erlooking Aylesbury's vale,
On to the Chiltern Downs,
  Rich in our island's tale.

In our village churchyard is her grave,
   Where, after sharp fever and pain,
We laid her to rest, and gave
   Her soul ransomed to Jesu again.

Though *no* father or mother was there
   To join in the last sacred rite,
Dear relations and friends joined in prayer,
   Sad in the dull autumn light.

And her schoolmates and teachers, who knew
   The child's worth or in *work* or in *play*,
Came from far, her grave to bestrew
   With flowers, their last offering to pay.

A good Bishop* from o'er the South Sea
   With his brethren counsel to take
Came home, and willing he
   For ' auld lang syne's ' friendship's sake

In India; at our own request
   Our loved Church's sacred rite
Of confirmation held, and blessed
   The young children robed in white.

   *   *   *   *   *

  * The Bishop of Auckland was twice decorated for service
in the Mutiny, once after Lucknow, and again after the
Umbeylah or Black Mountain campaign; the author and the
Bishop were at the adjoining stations of Shajahanpur and
Bareilly, and the author was afterwards chaplain of Bareilly.
The two friends had not met for twenty-three years.

And Minnie she was one of these
  On whom he laid his hands,
Meekly kneeling on her knees
  Amongst the white-clothed bands.

Two clergymen had watched and prayed
  For her at home and school,
And readily her mind obeyed
  The Church's law and rule,

So reverently with those loved best
  In sweet communion came,
Obedient to her Lord's behest,
  His promised *life* to claim.

For she believed that those who eat
  *In faith** His body given,
And drank his blood, He'd ne'er forget,
  But write their names in heaven.

The clergymen who trained her soul
  In spirit to seek God,
In vain their tears tried to control
  As they laid her 'neath the sod.

And turning from the green grave's brink
  One thus to the other said,
I ne'er knew one so young deep drink
  Of God's spirit as this maid.'

  * After a heavenly and spiritual manner.

Only a child, and yet so keen
   And vivid was her sight
Of things above that the veiled unseen
   To her seemed full of light.

     *   *   *   *   *

L'ENVOY.

Loved ones have placed, with tender care,
   O'er her grave a pure white cross,
But her soul has soared to the heavenly air,
   To her *gain* we know, but our loss.

FAREWELL TO SIR HUGH ROSE, K.C.B., AFTERWARDS LORD STRATHNAIRN.

'He was a man, take him for all in all, we shall not look upon his like again.'

OUR Chief has gone! a soldier good
   As e'er in battles fought;
For none than he have sturdier stood
   Where dangers could be sought.
God speed him on his homeward way
And land him safe from Dublin's Bay.*

* Sir Hugh was appointed Commander-in-Chief of the Forces in Ireland in the Fenian troubles.

In India long will live his *name*,
  His deeds few will forget;
And many a tongue shall sound his fame
  Of those unborn as yet;
Who to the rescue came from far
When fierce roll'd on the tide of war.

The days were dark in fifty-seven,
  E'en stout hearts quailed with fear,
And a long, deep wail rose up to Heaven,
  For little help seemed near;
And rare was nerve and head and hand
The subtle natives to withstand!

And only here and there a man
  Fit for *chief* rank was found,
To rule, to guide, or shape a plan,
  And offer counsel sound:
Fit for the times up *rose* Sir Hugh
When others faltered, firm and true.

To Cawnpore up, from far Bombay,
  With heroes brave on prest,
Through the angry torrent forced his way,
  Nor thought of peace or rest,
Till he had fought, and not in vain,
The Central Indian campaign.

Nor burning heat, nor deadly stroke*
 Of noonday's glaring sun,
Our hero's iron spirit broke;
 He toiled till all was won,
Nor sheathed his sword till dusky foe
Lay prostrate 'neath its crushing blow.

And those who saw the work well done,
 To talk of its *dash* ne'er tire—
How to the front he wheeled each gun,
 And oped a withering fire,
Or how the cavalry pursued,
And foemen right and left down-hewed!

And when the bitter strife was o'er,
 And perfect peace restored;
When men went forth to fight no more,
 And sheathed was sharpened sword,
The weal of those who with him bled
The Chief full well rememberèd :†

The soldier found him his best friend
 His welfare to promote;
To his wants a willing ear he'd lend,
 To his cause his heart devote:

---

* Sir Hugh was twice in this campaign thrown from his horse by sunstroke.

† It was the great desire of his heart to provide better barracks for the men; and this he succeeded in doing. His best act was, perhaps, in diminishing the rum ration.

Comrades in warfare bless the day
When first o'er them Sir Hugh held sway.

Farewell, brave Chief; e'en now we need
   Thy counsel and thy skill in arms;
But thou hast won of praise thy meed,
   And England waits thee with her charms;
And thither rightly should be turned
The warrior's steps, to honours nobly earned.

THE END.

Elliot Stock, Paternoster Row. London.

www.ingramcontent.com/pod-product-compliance
Lightning Source LLC
Chambersburg PA
CBHW032349020726
47499CB00008B/2674